Invasion Force: Microbe

Written by Quentin Flynn
Illustrated by Russell Tate

Contents

1 Emergency Evacuation 4
2 Be Prepared 11
3 Invasion Underway 18
4 Under Attack 24
5 A Dreaded Enemy 31
6 Heavy Casualties 38
7 Never Surrender 44

For learning solutions, visit cengage.com.au

Meet the Characters

S Battalion

A bacterial invasion force.

Lieutenant Colonel Spittle

The commander of S Battalion.

Major Phlegming

An officer in S Battalion.

Enemy T-cells

A type of white blood cell.

Enemy B-cells

Another type of white blood cell.

Enemy Macrophages and Neutrophils

Other white blood cells.

Dear Reader

Getting a sore throat is no fun. When tiny bacterial microbes invade our bodies, they usually make us feel very unwell – until our immune system starts to fight back! It's amazing to think that, for almost every type of bacteria, there's a single white blood cell with the unique ability to fight it. All our bodies have to do is find the right one!

Quentin Flynn
Author

Invasion Map

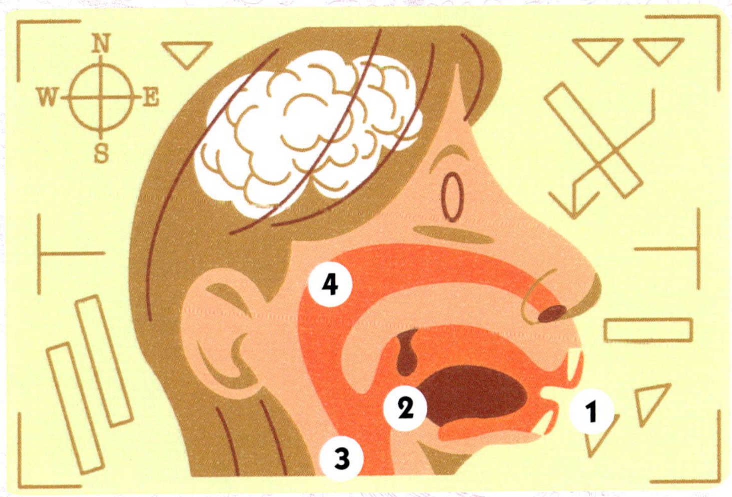

1. Entry point (mouth)
2. Invasion point (scratched skin)
3. Battle site (throat)
4. Secondary battle site (nasal passage)

1 Emergency Evacuation

After three days of dangerous combat, the order to move out finally arrived. The last twelve hours of bitter fighting and heavy casualties had taken their toll on every one of us: me, my commanding officer and our weary troops.

We were S Battalion, part of an invasion force facing a relentless enemy attack. In the face of overwhelming numbers and superior weapons, our dire situation had worsened by the hour.

Now, the choice we faced was stark. Abandon our position – or face death at the hands of our merciless foes.

0930 HRS INVASION DAY +3. TOP SECRET.

TO: CO, S BATTALION

FROM: GENERAL SNIFFLE-KOFF

DECISION TAKEN TO ABANDON INVASION DUE TO OVERWHELMING ENEMY FORCES. NO REINFORCEMENTS AVAILABLE. WITHDRAW IMMEDIATELY FROM ALL POSITIONS AND ACTIVATE EMERGENCY EVACUATION PLANS. REGRET S BATTALION IS ON ITS OWN. GOOD LUCK.

Within seconds of receiving the order from General Sniffle-Koff, my commanding officer, or "CO", Lieutenant Colonel Spittle, swung into action.

"Major Phlegming!" he yelled. "Give me an urgent situation report."

"It's bad," I confirmed. "Since the battalion first saw action in Operation Delta Echo Romeo Echo Kilo, we've lost around half our strength. We're down to about 300 infantry. We can rebuild, but it'll take time, and we don't have that. We're surrounded, and we've had unconfirmed reports that a vast number of fresh enemy troops are heading this way."

"Tell our forces to get ready for immediate evacuation," ordered Lieutenant Colonel Spittle. "You know the plan, Phlegming. Assemble the battalion in one place and prepare to move out."

"Yes, sir!" I nodded. I wheeled around and raced for the front line, barking orders as I went. I knew that time was against us and if I was too slow, our entire battalion would be annihilated.

Less than a minute later, the survivors of our once strong S Battalion found themselves fighting a desperate rearguard action. Evacuation meant assembling in one location – and, for a few deadly moments, that meant the full force of the enemy was focused upon us.

"Wait for my command," hollered Lieutenant Colonel Spittle. "Wait for it!"

Suddenly, there was a lull in the fighting as the enemy gathered its strength for one final attack.

"Now!" shouted the commanding officer.

Simultaneously, every member of S Battalion fell to the ground, bracing themselves for the inevitable. One second passed. Two seconds.

And then, just as Lieutenant Colonel Spittle had hoped, there was a gigantic convulsion, roaring like a massive earthquake.

"Here we go!" shouted Lieutenant Colonel Spittle above the roar of the impending chaos. "Remember! Stay together!"

"Sorry," croaked Derek, after his coughing fit had calmed down. "Sudden tickle in my throat."

"Are you sure you're OK?" asked his teacher, Mrs Morrison. "Do you need a drink of water?"

"No, it's just this sore throat," replied Derek glumly. "I've had it for three days now, but I'm slowly starting to feel better."

"Situation report!" barked Lieutenant Colonel Spittle.

I assessed the area we'd landed in. "Looks like a pencil," I reported. "We've landed on a pencil on a desk."

"Hmm," grunted the lieutenant colonel. We were both thinking the same thing. A pencil wasn't ideal – but it was better than being overwhelmed by enemy forces with only one possible outcome.

"Most of the troops have made it, but we'll need water, sustenance and a warm environment. And we'll need it fast," I said. "This pencil has a hard, non-porous surface. At least we're not at risk of direct sunlight – but I'd give us an hour at the most."

Lieutenant Colonel Spittle knew he had to rally his troops. After narrowly escaping a terrible defeat, he needed to keep morale up.

"I won't lie to you," he said, addressing the remnants of his battalion. "Some of you won't make it." There was a murmur amongst the survivors of S Battalion. "Things are tough – and, as this pencil starts drying out, things will get tougher."

The faces of his loyal soldiers looked grim. Grim, but determined.

"But we're tough too," said Lieutenant Colonel Spittle, raising his voice. "And I know that no matter how long we're marooned on this pencil, as long as there's one member of S Battalion left, this proud invasion force will carry on its mission!"

"Yes, sir!" shouted a voice from the assembled troops, to a rumble of assent.

"S Battalion will never surrender!" cried the lieutenant colonel. "Remember our motto!"

"Infection, infection, infection!" thundered the voices of the troops.

The lieutenant colonel turned to me. "Now we wait, Phlegming," he murmured. "Let's hope it won't be too long."

"Yes, sir," I replied. The commanding officer and I settled down. We'd made it out of Delta Echo Romeo Echo Kilo alive. But there was no anticipating what the future held.

2 Be Prepared

Twenty minutes into that future, Lieutenant Colonel Spittle of S Battalion turned to me with a concerned look on his face. "How are the troops faring, Major?"

"I'm getting unconfirmed reports of severe evaporation around the edges of our enclave," I reported. "The troops are huddling together to save valuable moisture, but I don't know how long we can hold out here."

"No signs of any disinfectant?" asked Lieutenant Colonel Spittle. "No reports of soap?"

"Nothing so far," I responded, glad to offer some good news.

"Excellent," said Lieutenant Colonel Spittle, with a sigh of relief. "At the moment, we need all the good news we can get. Tell the troops to maintain their state of readiness. We might have to move at any second. We need to be prepared."

“Yes, sir,” I nodded, hurrying off to relay the lieutenant colonel’s orders to my remaining battalion members.

“Hey, Derek, can I borrow your pencil?” asked Amber. Derek frowned at Amber, the girl who insisted on sitting next to him in class. She was forever lending her pencils to other kids and forgetting to get them back.

“OK,” Derek agreed reluctantly. “But don’t lose it, like the other hundred you’ve already lost this term.”

“Thanks,” grinned Amber. “I won’t. By the way, your sore throat sounds like it’s getting better.”

“At least I’ve stopped coughing and spluttering everywhere,” agreed Derek.

Another ten minutes passed. We had, at best, thirty minutes left.

“Update,” said Lieutenant Colonel Spittle.

"Evaporation still a concern," I said. "Temperature's dropped to about 20 degrees Celsius. Still manageable."

"There's nothing for it," observed my commanding officer. "We'll just have to sit tight and hope that ..."

Without warning, we were plunged into darkness. The lieutenant colonel's voice reverberated throughout the inky blackness.

"Wait for it, troops," he shouted, sounding instantly alert. "This looks like zero hour for a new invasion!"

Amber stared at the maths problem on the whiteboard at the front of the class.

"What's your answer?" she whispered, leaning over towards Derek.

"Don't get too close," hissed Derek. "You might catch my bugs."

Amber sat back. Like most people, she thought that bacteria were passed mainly through the air. But she was wrong. She stared at the maths problem. It was a tough one. She twiddled the pencil in her hand. And then, deciding she needed to retrieve her calculator from her bag, she popped the pencil in her mouth, and opened her bag with both hands.

Seconds later, I heard the commanding officer of S Battalion calling out to me. "Phlegming! Are you there? How many of us made it?"

I was wet and sticky. I wiped myself down as best I could and peered through the shadowy darkness. "I can make out about two hundred of us, sir."

"Two hundred, eh?" whistled Lieutenant Colonel Spittle. "That's not as many as I'd hoped, but it should be enough. Give me a situation rcport."

"All indications are positive, sir," I responded. My microbial training kicked into action, and I surveyed my immediate environment for threats. "Acidity and viscosity consistent with saliva, sir.

It's mildly antibacterial, sir, but not strong enough to deal with us. Temperature about 37 degrees Celsius."

"Hmm," said the lieutenant colonel thoughtfully. "Things are looking up, Major. It's about half a degree cooler than ears, eyes or nasal passages. That means we're in a mouth."

"Yes, sir," I agreed, allowing myself the faintest of smiles.

"Tell the troops to take up defensive positions near the rear of the cavity," ordered Lieutenant Colonel Spittle, checking his wristwatch. "10 00 hours. We should be safe from mouthwash until at least 13 00 hours – up to 19 00 hours if we're fortunate and our host doesn't brush and rinse until after dinner. Burrow in deep, avoid getting trapped in mucus and swallowed, and post some lookouts, just in case."

"Yes, sir," I replied.

"And once the troops are in position, give out the order for some well-deserved 'R and R'," added the battalion commander. "That's long overdue."

“Yes, sir,” I nodded emphatically. I knew the troops would welcome some Rest and Replication after the events of the last few hours. The members of S Battalion would double in numbers every twenty minutes. In an hour, our battalion would find itself returned to full strength – 1 600 fighting fit members, ready for action.

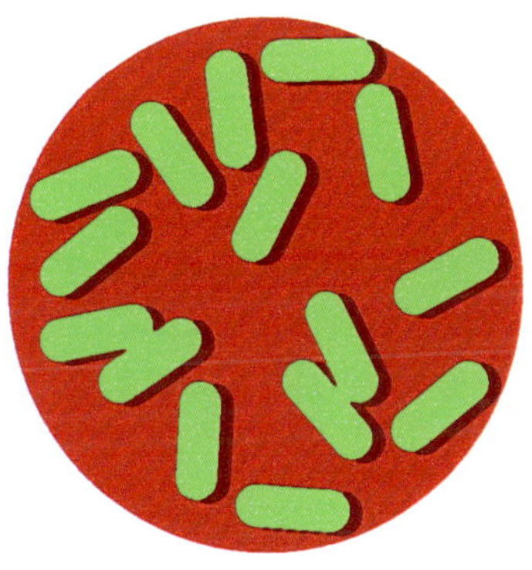

3 Invasion Underway

Sixty minutes had passed since zero hour. Z+1. I'd waited quietly as the hour passed, watchful for any threats. Our chances of detection were low, but we still had to exercise caution. We needed to regroup and build our strength up for the next phase of Operation Alfa Mike Bravo Echo Romeo. Soon enough, the battalion was ready.

"Over here," called Lieutenant Colonel Spittle. He'd been exploring the perimeter of our encampment and he'd found exactly what he'd been searching for. A fragment of skin had been scratched, probably by something our host had eaten. Beneath it, I could see an inviting network of broken capillaries.

"Looks like our luck's in," I said to the CO. "I'll rouse the troops as unobtrusively as I can."

It didn't take long before the battalion was assembled, eager to embark on the next phase of our invasion.

Lieutenant Colonel Spittle kept a close eye on the capillaries. “Normal white blood cell traffic. We’ll start taking casualties as soon as we’re in, but we’ve got the advantage of numbers. No sign of T-cells or ... you know who,” he whispered. “Give the order!”

“Go, go, go!” I yelled, directing the troops to launch their invasion. Like highly trained paratroopers jumping in orderly formation, a determined cascade of microbes forced their way between the thin cell walls of the capillaries. As soon as the last of the troops disappeared, I jumped too, closely followed by Lieutenant Colonel Spittle.

A little over an hour after the commencement of Alfa Mike Bravo Echo Romeo, we were in.

“Infection underway!” I beamed at the CO.

“Well done, troops,” boomed Lieutenant Colonel Spittle. “Now, let’s take advantage of the situation, while we’re still unnoticed.”

It was a good call. The masses of red blood cells rushing past were oblivious to our presence – and

there were nutrients aplenty in the warm, rich lymph in which we were all bathed.

"Remember, troops, don't get carried away by the lymph," I warned. "You'll end up getting eliminated in the lymph nodes. And I don't want to hear of anyone becoming trapped in the spleen. Its only job is to detect foreign cells, and this battalion can't afford to set off alarm bells just yet."

"Yes, sir!" echoed the 1 600 members of S Battalion.

Conditions were perfect for another hour of undisturbed replication – but I knew from my extensive microbial training that it wouldn't last. Capillaries, like every blood vessel, were full of patrolling neutrophils. These kamikaze white blood cells engulfed any foreign microbes they came across, killing the invader and themselves with deadly enzymes. Fortunately, the numbers were with us. For every member of S Battalion we lost to a neutrophil, there'd be another 1 599 replicating themselves. It was a war of attrition – but for the next 48 hours, we'd be able to replicate faster than they could knock us out. I pressed between two capillary wall cells, out of the direct path of any neutrophils patrolling our territory.

"Sir!" I hissed urgently. "Sir! Wake up!"

An hour had passed since the battalion had busied themselves by doubling every 20 minutes. We'd taken some hits – but I'd hardened myself to the sight of individual troops being picked off by neutrophils. Constant warfare does that to you. A handful of macrophages, greedy white blood cells that consumed the dead neutrophils and our unfortunate comrades, were busily cleaning up around the perimeter of the encampment. The troops were determinedly dividing in two, unaware of the imminent danger I'd just spotted heading in our direction.

"What is it?" croaked the lieutenant colonel, shaking himself awake.

I pointed upstream, and the CO sat bolt upright.

"Lymphocyte!" he breathed, recognising the worst kind of white blood cell. "Is it a T-cell or ...?" There were two kinds of lymphocyte – but not even the CO could bring himself to utter the name of the other, our most feared enemy.

Produced in the thymus, a small organ in the chest of our host, T-cells were killer white blood cells. They were the stormtroopers of the white blood cell army, and they had a fearsome reputation. They not only ruthlessly killed invaders; they killed any of the host cells we were caught hiding in, just to be certain. You didn't want to mess with a T-cell – but they weren't as bad as the other lymphocyte.

"Identity confirmed," I replied. "T-cell."

"Full defensive positions," yelled Lieutenant Colonel Spittle at the top of his voice. "We've had it easy up until now, troops, but Operation Alfa Mike Bravo Echo Romeo is about to start getting nasty!"

He wasn't wrong. At Z+2, the battle was about to heat up. Literally.

4 Under Attack

With the arrival of the T-cell, the mood in the surrounding tissue changed. We were on full alert – but the macrophages consuming the bodies of our valiant fallen troops snapped to attention too. T-cells demanded respect, not only from their enemies, but from their own side.

The T-cell pushed itself roughly against one of the macrophages. I could imagine the conversation.

"Hey, watch where you're going," the macrophage would say, before recognising the grim killer white blood cell.

"What have you got there?" the T-cell would demand.

"Sorry, sir. Just found a microbe," would come the reply. "But I've dealt with it. There's not much left."

"Hand it over, soldier," would come the order. The T-cell would check the cellular code of the remains. If they matched those of the host, it'd move on. No danger.

I knew in my heart that wouldn't happen. Every human being had his or her own unique code – and it was different to ours. The instant the T-cell examined the remains, it'd discover a code it had never come across before. T-cells weren't allowed any discretion: if the code didn't match the host, it was automatically a foreigner. An unwelcome invader. And the T-cell's reaction would be swift and merciless.

Lieutenant Colonel Spittle had seen this happen enough times to know that things were about to get serious. "What's our battalion strength?" he hissed.

"Latest estimates are about 3 200, more or less," I replied. "We've established infections in most of the surrounding tissue. The troops have met little resistance when moving through cell walls. Even with a T-cell prowling around, we'll still get to over 6 000 by Z+3. One T-cell can only inflict so much damage."

"It can't replicate fast enough to deal with all of us, and there's only one way that it can call in reinforcements," snapped the CO. He pointed to the capillary. "This is a one-way flow, and it's pretty tight.

At best, white blood cells can move a millimetre every minute. But this leads to a vein, and once our friend over there makes it into the main circulation system, it'll take 60 seconds at most to get right around the host's body, alerting reinforcements."

"Our best chance is to delay the white blood cells as long as we can, right here," I said.

"We need to clog this capillary and slow them down," said the CO grimly. "That's going to mean ..."

"I know, sir. The only way to clog this capillary is with bodies," I said. "We need a suicide squad."

"It'll buy us enough time for the other troops to replicate even more," said the CO.

"I'll send out the request," I said, gritting my teeth. Sometimes, in the heat of battle, terrible decisions had to be made. This was one of them.

I could barely bring myself to watch as a squad of my valiant comrades made their way out of the cell walls where they'd been hiding and swarmed around the T-cell. Surely enough, while we'd been talking, it had detected a foreign cell code, and that had set off an immediate reaction. The T-cell itself was replicating as rapidly as it could. Two, then four, then eight, then sixteen killer white blood cells attacked the squad from S Battalion with fatal consequences.

We took heavy casualties, but within half an hour, we'd limited the enemy's capabilities. Lieutenant Colonel Spittle's decision had been the right one. The battlefield was crowded with dead T-cells and the bodies of our own forces. Macrophages further clogged the narrow capillary, moving in to clear up the carnage. The few remaining T-cells tried to push through the capillary, but found it difficult to move out of the area.

"Situation report, Major!" called the CO from his position in one of the cells lining the capillary walls.

"Engagement with the enemy successful, sir," I called back. I checked the other members of S Battalion. "R and R proceeding to plan."

I took a deep breath. And then the enemy threw something at us I hadn't expected so soon.

Interleukin. The macrophages started secreting the hormone known as interleukin.

"Is that what I think it is, Major?" shouted the CO.

I gritted my teeth and nodded.

"Blast," said the CO. "This enemy's a clever one.

That stuff will go round the bloodstream faster than any white blood cell."

"Straight to the hypothalamus," I said grimly.

"I'm boiling! It's getting really hot in here, don't you think?" asked Amber. She took off her jacket.

Derek looked up from the module of work he was working his way through. "All the windows are open," he said. "Feels fine to me."

There was nothing we could do to halt the stream of interleukin hormones heading for the nearest vein. Once there, the hormones would be pushed towards the heart and pumped out into an artery. Even a trace entering the artery leading to the hypothalamus, deep within the host's brain, would spell an end to our delaying tactics. Temperature regulation.

That's what the hypothalamus did. At the slightest trace of interleukin, the hypothalamus would immediately raise the body's temperature. Not only would that make the blood vessels, including our capillary, grow wider, making it easier for the surviving T-cells to escape and alert more white blood cells, it would also make life more uncomfortable for S Battalion. In temperatures between 37 and 38 degrees Celsius, we could replicate and flourish. Anything hotter than that, and the troops were forced to slow down.

The host was about to come down with a high temperature. A fever, which would feel terrible – but it was the body's way of throwing another obstacle in our path. The enemy had outfoxed us.

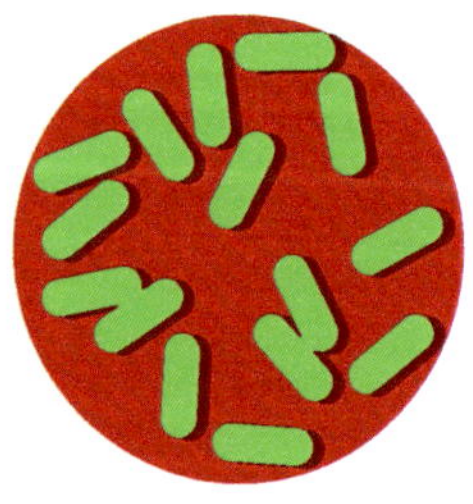

5 A Dreaded Enemy

By Z+4, I was sweating with heat exhaustion. Like all battles, this was a numbers game, and the enemy numbers were increasing by the minute. With the dilation of the blood vessels, a few T-cells had squeezed through, and managed to escape into a vein. The reinforcements they'd urgently called for raced to the scene of the infection.

Hidden deep within the surrounding tissue, S Battalion did their best to continue replicating, despite the uncomfortable temperatures. We were still making gains, but it was nowhere near where we needed to be. The T-cell forces were still fewer than we were; but they replicated much more rapidly and their presence brought swarms of neutrophils and macrophages to the scene.

Worse still, the widening of the blood vessels meant that the host's immune system could send in the thing we'd all been dreading.

“Keep your eyes peeled,” warned Lieutenant Colonel Spittle. “We need to watch their every move.”

“Yes, sir,” I said, eyes darting across the battlefield. And then I saw them.

“Sir,” I said. The CO followed my outstretched hand with his gaze and a dark look engulfed his face.

“B-cells,” he breathed, finally giving voice to the words that no one ever wanted to hear. He shook his head in despair.

Over generations, humans had evolved to fight off invasions from microbes such as S Battalion using an amazing system. Within each human, there was perhaps a million white blood cells, all different, all waiting for their moment of glory. Each one carried a tiny strand of protein exactly matched to just one kind of microbe. If the white blood cell found a match, it released a chemical poison, which targetted only the microbes with that protein.

Somewhere, hidden amongst the ten trillion cells that made up this human, lay a B-Cell with the cellular code to destroy us all. It might take a million attempts, but eventually, this human would find the right B-cell. Then that B-cell would replicate repeatedly, until our forces were overwhelmed. Operation Alfa Mike Bravo Echo Romeo would be finished.

Millimetre by millimetre, the B-cells approached. Lieutenant Colonel Spittle and I watched them nervously. They moved ghoulishly through the wreckage of the battlefield, meticulously checking the remains of the bodies they found one by one, trying to match them against the cellular code programmed into them. They drew closer, sampling their environment, searching for a key that would unleash their devastating effects.

"Surely this advance party won't contain the one, sir," I whispered to the CO. "That would be incredibly bad luck."

000100
010010
001100
010100
111011
000100

"It's like Russian roulette," growled the lieutenant colonel. "You never know when your number's up."

The first B-cell prowled past. Our luck seemed to be holding. For now.

"There'll be another one," observed the CO soberly as it moved past us and disappeared back into the bloodstream beyond. "And another. They never give up until they find the right one."

"I don't feel so good," said Amber, when her mother picked her up after school. "I've been hot all day, and now I'm starting to feel tired."

"That's no good," replied her mother. She held a hand against Amber's forehead. "You do feel hot," she said. "I hope you're not coming down with something."

We held onto our positions for another seven long hours, desperately trying to replicate faster than the T-cells, the neutrophils and the macrophages that could destroy us. At Z+11, our morale was still strong. We'd had a head start in the replication race, and things could still go either way. Lieutenant Colonel Spittle and I decided that S Battalion had sufficient troops to split up and infect different areas along the front line. We had squads positioned in the nasal passage, the throat, the eyes, and had sent some heavily armed scouts down into the lungs. We knew that if we spread ourselves out, the enemy would have to split their troops, too. With any luck, we'd get the upper hand in an area that had a weaker concentration of white blood cells.

But, as we were soon to find out, luck wasn't to be on our side in Operation Alfa Mike Bravo Echo Romeo. At Z+12, the host found a new ally. One that could change the final outcome of this battle.

"Make sure Amber takes one of these every four hours," said the doctor, writing out a prescription. "A course of antibiotics should stop a bacterial infection getting worse. Hopefully, we'll have it cleared up in no time."

Amber's mother collected the bottle of antibiotics from the dispensary of the after-hours clinic, and headed back home.

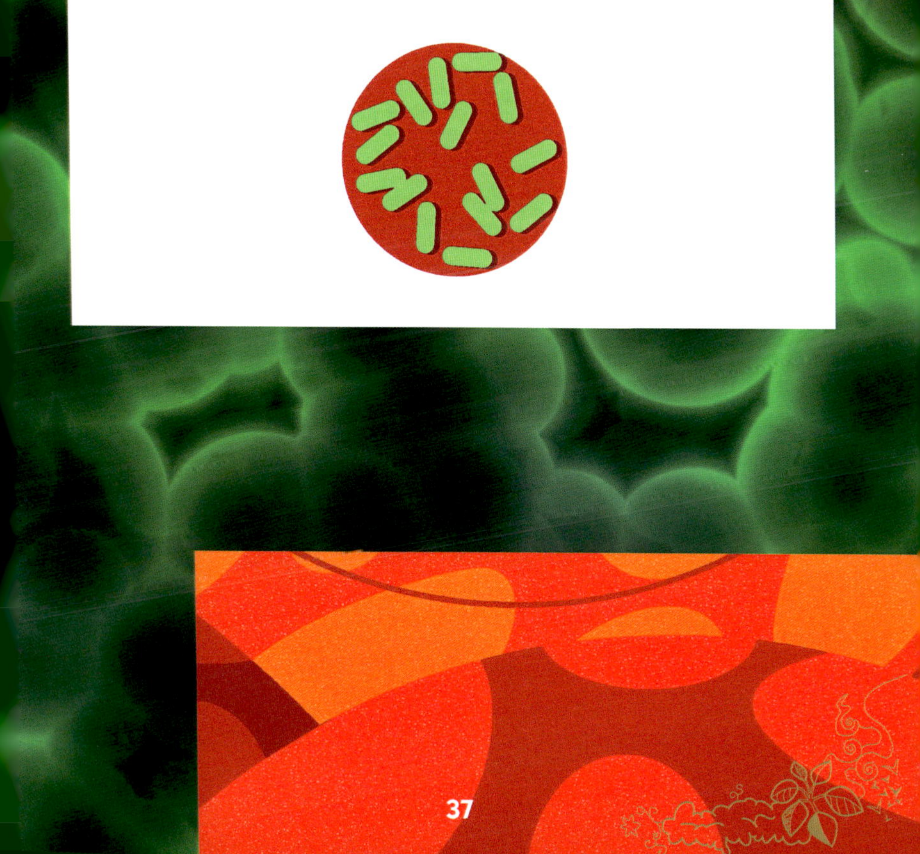

6 Heavy Casualties

At Z+12, the antibiotic hit us. It didn't kill us – but it did something worse. Antibiotics work by preventing us from replicating. And without R and R, we'd simply be picked off, one by one, by the T-cells, neutrophils and macrophages. It might take a week, but it was simple mathematics. Without the ability to replicate in huge numbers, we'd eventually be overwhelmed.

There was a slight glimmer of hope, however, and Lieutenant Colonel Spittle seized upon it.

"Have each of the platoons and companies report back to me with a full update of replication rates. I want to know about anything unusual."

"Resistance," I smiled, with a look of steely resolve. "Humans have been using antibiotics so much that the strongest amongst us have developed resistance."

"Exactly," replied the CO. "Find out which of our troops are still replicating. We'll group the resistant fighters together and launch a counterattack."

The next two hours saw us taking some heavy casualties. The antibiotic slowed our replication rate down to a trickle. The T-cells continued their merciless onslaught – but they could only kill us one at a time. If enough of our troops had resistance, our numbers might just continue to increase. It'd be slow. But at Z+14, it was our best chance.

The macrophages were finding so many dead bodies to clean up that they couldn't cope. The host started producing masses of sticky phlegm and mucus to slow us down. Dead kamikaze neutrophils and the remains of microbes, slaughtered by marauding T-cells, mixed with the mucus. The result was a thick, gooey mess.

"Hold on, troops!" I shouted, as I felt the first tremors of another coughing fit. With each convulsion, we lost even more troops, flung to the outside world in a spray of mucus and phlegm.

A steady stream of B-cells flowed through the capillary, each of them trying to match their unique cellular code with ours. By Z+15, we must have seen thousands of them. But so far, none of them had been the one.

I'd gathered up as many of the resistant troops as I could muster. I led them over to where Lieutenant Colonel Spittle was directing his remaining troops.

"Troops," he said, surveying the tough-looking microbes I'd assembled. "The success of Operation Alfa Mike Bravo Echo Romeo depends upon you."

One of the resistant fighters spoke up. "We're ready, sir. No antibiotic's going to stop us!"

"That's the spirit," replied the CO. "Now I want you to spread out in small groups. Search for places where the enemy will never find you. Go for major organs. If we can make the host feel as miserable as possible, we can weaken their defences. Get ready to move out!"

The resistant fighters snapped to attention and saluted the commanding officer.

"Yes, sir!" they shouted defiantly. "We won't let you down, sir."

They didn't stand a chance. Resistant or not, they had no defences against the lethal threat that was making its way down the capillary. I don't know who saw it first, me or the lieutenant colonel. But when we did, we knew our mission was doomed.

It was a B-cell. It looked just like all the rest. But when its cellular code found an exact match in one of our battalion's soldiers, we saw the B-cell start to replicate. The human's immune system had found what it had been searching for.

Lieutenant Colonel Spittle and I watched in horror as the B-cell split to form two; then four; then eight. And then each B-cell started secreting a deadly chemical weapon against which we had no defences. Antibodies, specifically designed to kill members of S Battalion and only S Battalion, started to flow into the blood system.

T-cells continued their killer onslaught. Neutrophils engulfed microbes. The hypothalamus, flooded with interleukin produced by millions of busily cleaning macrophages, kept the temperature

climbing. Antibiotics swirled through the blood vessels, keeping our troops in check. And the rapidly dividing B-cells released wave after wave of poisonous antibodies into the bloodstream.

At Z+16, I couldn't stand it any longer. The situation was futile.

"Lieutenant Colonel Spittle," I yelled. "S Battalion can't take much more of this. We're surrounded and outgunned. It's only a matter of time before all positions are overrun. What are your orders, sir? What are your orders?"

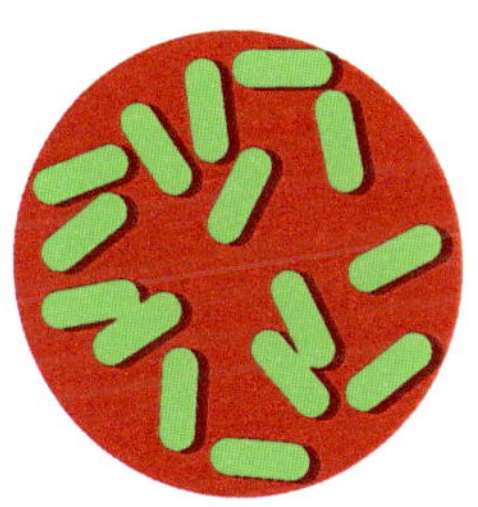

7 Never Surrender

It was Delta Echo Romeo Echo Kilo all over again! After sixteen hours of dangerous combat, Lieutenant Colonel Spittle knew the situation was hopeless. The combined forces of the T-cells, the B-cells and the antibiotics were simply too much for S Battalion. He gave the order to get ready to move out.

We were all exhausted after so much bitter fighting. We'd sustained heavy casualties. The CO and I, along with the troops who'd survived, fought our way to the evacuation point. Despite our heroic efforts, every one of us knew we had little choice: we had to abandon our position or face death at the hands of our merciless foes.

"Do I have to go to school?" pleaded Amber the next morning. "I'm tired and I've got a sore throat."

"The doctor said that if you take those antibiotics, whatever it is will clear up in no time," replied her mother. "It's probably not serious – nothing worth skipping school for."

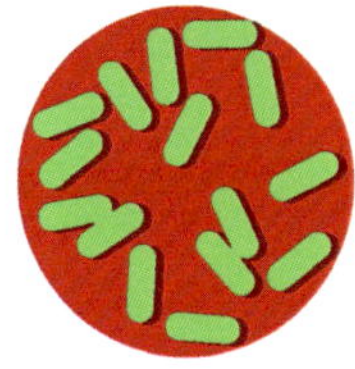

"Troops of S Battalion," roared the CO, addressing the assembled microbes. "We're about to leave our last remaining stronghold. I don't know where we'll end up. Perhaps a handkerchief, a lunchbox lid or the handrail of an escalator. Who knows?"

The handful of surviving troops who were facing an uncertain future fell silent.

"But what I do know," continued the CO, "is that S Battalion will survive. As long as there's one of us left, we will never surrender. And we will never be beaten."

A spontaneous cheer arose from the ranks.

"Get ready for immediate evacuation," ordered Lieutenant Colonel Spittle. "You all know the drill. Operation Alfa Mike Bravo Echo Romeo is at an end."

Less than a minute later, the survivors of our once-strong S Battalion found themselves again fighting a desperate rearguard action. For a few deadly moments, the full force of the enemy was focused upon us.

"Wait for my command," hollered Lieutenant Colonel Spittle. "Wait for it!"

Suddenly, there was a lull in the fighting as the enemy gathered its strength for one final attack.

"Now!" shouted the commanding officer. Simultaneously, every member of S Battalion fell to the ground, bracing ourselves as we'd done before. One second passed. Two seconds.

Amber reluctantly climbed out of the car and headed for the classroom. She supposed her mother was right. She'd be fine. And it would be a shame to miss out on seeing all her friends.

I waited for the cough. I had no idea what the future held. But I did know this war wasn't over. And I knew that Lieutenant Colonel Spittle was right.

Enough of us would survive to carry on the next battle. We'd launch another invasion. And I knew that because there was one thing S Battalion could always count on: someone, somewhere was about to touch something. Someone just like you.

Organisations involved in aviation, defence and emergency response use a phonetic alphabet to clearly transmit important messages. Instead of using letters of the alphabet, which may be misunderstood by the person needing the information, an agreed list of words is used to communicate each letter of the alphabet.

A: Alfa
B: Bravo
C: Charlie
D: Delta
E: Echo
F: Foxtrot
G: Golf
H: Hotel
I: India
J: Juliet
K: Kilo
L: Lima
M: Mike
N: November
O: Oscar
P: Papa
Q: Quebec
R: Romeo
S: Sierra
T: Tango
U: Uniform
V: Victor
W: Whiskey
X: X-ray
Y: Yankee
Z: Zulu